The Wheels on the Bus

and

The Boat on the Waves

Notes for adults

TADPOLES ACTION RHYMES are structured to provide support for
newly independent readers. The books may also be used by adults for
sharing with young children.

The language of action rhymes is often already familiar to an emergent
reader, so the opportunity to see these rhymes in print gives a highly
supportive early reading experience.

The alternative rhymes extend this reading experience further, and
encourage children to play with language and try out their own rhymes.

If you are reading this book with a child, here are a few suggestions:

1. Make reading fun! Choose a time to read when you and the child are
   relaxed and have time to share the story.

2. Recite the rhyme together before you start reading. What might the
   alternative rhyme be about? Why might the child like it?

3. Encourage the child to reread the rhyme, and to retell it in their
   own words, using the illustrations to remind them what has happened.

4. Point out together the repeated words on pages 12 and 22 (developing
   phonological awareness will help with decoding) and encourage the child
   to make up their own alternative rhymes and accompanying actions.

5. Give praise! Remember that small mistakes need not always be corrected.

First published in 2010 by
Franklin Watts
338 Euston Road
London NW1 3BH

Franklin Watts Australia
Level 17/207 Kent Street
Sydney NSW 2000

Text (Ride, Ride, Ride Your Bike)
© Wes Magee 2010
Illustration © Richard Morgan 2010

The rights of Wes Magee to be ident
the author of Ride, Ride, Ride Your
and Marina le Ray as the illustrator
Work have been asserted in accorda
with the Copyright, Designs and Pa
Act, 1988.

ISBN 978 0 7496 9367 1 (hbk)
ISBN 978 0 7496 9373 2 (pbk)

Series Editor: Melanie Palmer

The Wheels on the Bus

Retold by Wes Magee

Illustrated by Richard Morgan

FRANKLIN WATTS
LONDON • SYDNEY

Richard Morgan

"I thought it'd be fun to draw a bus in a tropical setting, with all the unusual animals that live there. Which ones can you spot?"

The wheels
on the bus go
round and round,

round and round,
round and round.

The wheels on
the bus go

round and round,

all day long.

The Wheels on the Bus

The wheels on the bus go

round and round,

round and round,

round and round.

The wheels on the bus go

round and round,

all day long.

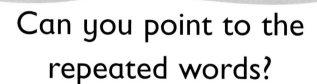

Can you point to the repeated words?

The Boat on the Waves

by Wes Magee
Illustrated by Richard Morgan

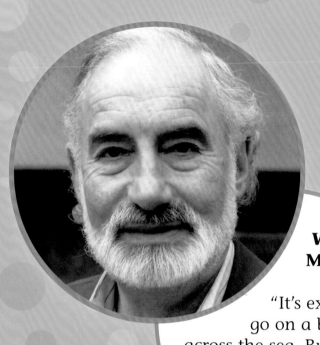

**Wes
Magee**

"It's exciting to
go on a boat trip
across the sea. But watch
out, the waves going up
and down can make
you seasick!"

The boat on the waves
goes up and down,

up and down,
up and down.

The boat on the
waves goes
up and down.

Splish! Splash! Splosh!

The Boat on the Waves

The boat on the waves

goes up and down,

up and down,

up and down.

The boat on the waves

goes up and down.

Splish! Splash! Splosh!

Can you point to the repeated words?

Puzzle Time!

How many boats can you
see in this picture?

Answers

There are 7 boats
in this picture.